The Unspoken

Book 1: The Reunion

ABUABAKAR M MARWA

authorHOUSE

AuthorHouse™ UK
1663 Liberty Drive
Bloomington, IN 47403 USA
www.authorhouse.co.uk
Phone: 0800.197.4150

Published by AuthorHouse 01/06/2016

ISBN: 978-1-5049-9783-6 (sc)
ISBN: 978-1-5049-9784-3 (hc)
ISBN: 978-1-5049-9785-0 (e)

Oxygen

There were no moons or stars in the night sky.

The air was still and cold, my fur stood on end, my body sensitized, ready for whatever would appear from this darkness.

I see one of the spots we have been looking for; a large gape we were shown through what they called satellite imagery, the hole was much larger, up close, a huge opening in the ground perfect in circumference.

By twelve I fall, twiggles unfurl, and I drop, they umbrella out allowing me to float in, I spin slowly in order to have a better vantage of my surroundings, I see nothing but a deep blackness, The place, is darker than the streets above, but I sense that I am in the right place. They call the things I hunt unspoken and their foot soldiers the shadow reapers. They are unlike any creature I had ever encountered; it is believed that they were conquerors of planets and creators of races, whom believe themselves, gods of this planet. They are stronger than their creation, the inhabitants of this blue spinning orb, but now they seem to have met their match. The reapers seemingly share a single consciousness, I gathered this from melding with one of them at quarantine while we were at the lunar station, it showed no form of independent thought, in fact the following words constantly echoed throughout its mind like a flowing stream "muluk wata tahawal" this in their tongue meant "conquer and transform". I believed that to be their primary mission objective.

As I approach the floor of this deep chasm I sense that I am not alone. They came in their thousands, and as they conquer the lands of this world by their strength and technology I fear they can do the same to others if they so choose. I gathered based on my prior encounters with the reapers that they do not have fear, my team and I have found that they gather in underground locations, we still don't know why they do not set up their bases above ground.

Our strategy since quarantine was to quietly infiltrate those areas and sanitize them one by one; we believed that we could quell the shadow reapers more easily one hole at a time. Before our arrival here cybers like ayeesha, were the main defense from any form of hostile aggression against her kind, but even though they were strong warriors and mounted a great defense they were losing ground to the reapers.

Since my team joined coupled with our own special skills and technology we have introduce a new and very different dimension to the fight.

I sense this is the location we were looking for I press the beacon on my left shoulder which should alert my team to make their way towards my location. I land very quietly, my feet firmly on the ground, the first thing I notice is how the air down here is less polluted than the air above ground, my breathing is much smoother the oxygen is not much unlike that on gruce untainted by whatever it was that made the air above ground so rancid.

Unbendable begins to hum its stone, which I call the eye; glows bright red, this happens when there are threats about. The glow from the stone shows me the vastness and the scale of this underground chasm. I see them now. I ground myself and recite the mantra "I fall by the power of twelve," my hearing becomes sharper I hear the shuffle of feet hurriedly yet cautiously approach my location, In seconds I am engaged by what felt like quite a number of the enemy, I stamp my right foot down with such force that the few around me are tossed away by the sheer magnitude of the shock wave created. I stand in the combative stance of 7, taught to me by lango lis after the death of my father, lango lis fed the wood to the flame of my desire to be a regimentarian just like him, he told me then this stance was known as the dance of death, it was Tekeshi kitanos most favorite combative movement. Spreading my feet apart and slowly bending down, I ground myself, and at the same time shout out to my sword "unbendable"!!! It unsheathes itself from behind me with immense speed and hovers only a few inches above me. Its stone shines bright red. I can now see my reflection in the dark brooding eyes of the enemy before me. I raise my right hand above my head and in a millisecond the handle of my ivory sword slides into its rightful place, the palm of my right hand, I clasp it tightly.

I attack on my toes moving with such speed that my feet only slightly touch the floor, time slows, I get to the first line of the enemy and open my sword hand unbendable flies above me and it spins and its distinctive whirling sound intensifies as its speed increases, it is music to my ears, as I engage the enemy with multiple strikes the dance has truly begun I then shout "kill" unbendable increases speed its pitch becomes higher, the stone then changes color from very bright red to a platinum fiery white.

Her voice " draemen save sum of them for us", she then says the other place they checked were decoys, I look above and I see nenveve, trool, and teek hovering above, my team has arrived. "Unbendable"!!! The sword seamlessly attaches itself to my open palm, as I clasp it shut around its warm handle, I see everything as clear as day the chasm is no longer dark, and I engage the enemy before me. With such speed, it appears to the reapers and those watching that I have mastered the art of teleportation, but it's only my speed of movement which makes it appear so. As I appear I strike with my left arm and slice with the sword cutting their bodies in half before they begin to fall, two three bodies at a time slicing, up and under decapitating these shadow reapers as I get my rhythm my strikes take four and five at a time, swinging to the left and right parrying at the enemy, absorbing their pulse rounds with my sword and also deflecting their fire and redirecting them back to their own kind. I have melded with them I know what they want to do and I preempt them. Any that stand before me death surely follows, the dance continues as I release the sword again it flies out of my hands and as tekeshis warriors of old I fight alongside my weapon, unbendable flies at the reapers and continues to do what It was made to, where it passes legs arms heads are severed. The population of the reapers begin to dwindle, they do not retreat or regroup they fight on even though it is a losing fight. From my periphery I can see the master psychomat at work, as she lands she simply makes solid movements with her hands and feet in form of the telekinetic katas, although she has eyes that see, she fights blind, and with every movement those that stand before her fall, they do not survive the injuries she inflicts on them, I can hear the breaking and shattering sounds of their very strong bones with every hand kata she performs in their direction, striking and slicing stamping on the floor and sweeping at the air in their direction, without a single physical touch nenveve inflicts death and destruction on the reapers. shoulders and elbows, knees hip joints blow apart, necks break, and brains liquefy oozing from their nasal cavities.

Trool the glory hogger swoops down fully morphed with twiggles sprouted, and begins his amazing movements, he lands on one leg and says "the shimmering lotus needs only a light touch to wilt" he stands on that leg as stable as an elder tree, as if to goad them into attacking him he remains on that leg throwing lightning fast spinning kicks, at the reapers both legs are never on the floor at the same time, he constantly kicks at the enemy, every kick lands on one reaper but due to the power behind them he inflicts damage on an average of six any of the enemy in his path dies, he turns and twists and with every movement strikes follow, his strikes are so solid hard that anything his fists, feet knees or elbows has contact with shatters, he is so quick and precise that he never misses a reaper every hit lands on target.

Teak our strategist, remains above us fully morphed with twiggles out. He uses an etherite pulse gun, a very effective tool in his hands, he collected it from the lunar base, it was given to him by ayeesha, he studied it and recalibrated it to his specific settings.

Teak inflicts more losses on the already quick dwindling number of the reapers. He curves his shots bending them so that one shot kills 4 or five at a time.

In very short order we find ourselves in the center of their corpses, "draemen let the etherite troops mop up, let them have a story to tell" I am still getting used to the meld, and how nenveve always manages to surprise me whenever she gives me instructions through the mind melding medium. I signal ayesha through our neck communicators, telling her that the coast was clear we four regimentarians had destroyed all the reapers in this hole. I still do not want them to know about how easily nenveve and I could invade their minds. I tell her to tell her cybers to follow her in chasm. They come in with their jet packs, the etherites are cerebral beings, for whatever power nature deprives them of having, they create or invent technologies that would replicate the same abilities, they are truly the masters of their environement.

She comes in with the troops, who finish off the few invaders left standing some are captured alive for interrogation and scientific study, without which we might never discover their true weaknesses and their true strengths, it is all a part of teaks plan of intelligence gathering. Nenveve and I have the ability to communicate with them. This is how we locate their subterranean bases more easily. The unspoken share one consciousness, they are linked by some kind of neural telepathic network, Nenveve and I possess the ability to invade their consciousness and tap into that network thus gaining knowledge of their aims and objectives.

"You are getting better Draemen", I reply back "thank you master", she then melds me another message "I am not your master; I am your friend, well done". Just then my mind went back to how this all started.

Flight

T he moons are all full, the night is as bright as day with a galaxy of stars dotting the distant sky. This marks the beginning of the winter. Ever slightly the bite of cold breeze blows on my face, while glancing at the moons through their mirror like reflection on the semi iced lake below. I think; tonight that experience, that feeling again, where my twiggles unfurl and expand according me the adventure of flight.

Now standing, at the location, one of the highest points we have at Bambush, a ridge atop a very tall hill called Scarfend, its name due to the fact the thundering wind at its summit forces our scarves to wave violently almost blowing them off our necks. The beat of my heart speeds up, that feeling again, it happens when blood pumps harder through my system forcing my twiggles to sprout. Only a hand full of us has this ability.

With the wind thundering on, I long for the sky and the taste of cool sweet cloud in my mouth, I never grow tired of its unrivalled taste and this place that I have come to for quite many a cycle. I mark the beginning of the Season here in my own special way.

The phosis begins. Taking a leap of faith, I drop, yelling out the words "I fall by the power of twelve". My velocity increases inch by inch as I fall, my muscles relax, my mind is in tune with the universe, the feeling, weightlessness overcomes me. It's great. My arms stretch out in front of me and my legs curl out behind me as the twiggles now fully engorged unfurl and begin to rotate, I gain altitude and the ground seems so far below as I rise above then dip my head and drop; velocity increases, my twiggles rotate faster lifting me. I again achieve altitude but at a faster speed. It's fantastic. Scarfend is below me. I repeat this movement over and over achieving blistering speeds. My abilities of flight aren't in doubt, in fact at the academy I was rated highly in technical flight. After about an hour of phosis maneuvers I begin my journey home. My dwelling is located by the hillside outside of the city, a location I love because of its serenity. It was my father's unit; I took charge of it after he had passed. I was his only son; my father was a morpher like me. We usually become regimentarians. He was a weilder regimentarian. Wielders were weapon masters, their skills were acquired by many cycles of dedication to training. My father was the last of the wielder class. In the academy they no longer teach weapon katas to cadets, the academy have a policy of not meddling with the metaphysical nature of wielding this is why within the core there are no longer wielders present, its practice has been phased out.

I see my home some distance ahead, my twiggles umbrella out and I begin a slow decent, I notice something out of the ordinary, there appears to be about a dozen bodies littered all over my land, and they weren't there earlier when I set off for Scarfend. I do a quick glancing fly by, I didn't notice any odd movements so I Immediately retracted my twiggles in order to quicken my descent, and I touched down in seconds, getting a better look at them. I realize They look very strange not like any beings I have ever come across they appear to be bi pedals like us but with little fur.

It is less cold here on the ground, but the snow is thick, these beings show no sign of bleeding or trauma to the body, they just lay still and lifeless.

Some movement and a faint voice from the bushes behind me, could it be that one of them still lives, running quickly in that direction, the sound of a loud blast pierces the cold silent air and the snow covered ground about two feet away from me bursts, instinct takes over and jumping up and away midflight my twiggles sprout taking me to the skies, in seconds, the farm is over 400 meters below me, the sense of danger abounds, who was that voice and why did it shoot at me, it must be hostile. That was a strong and powerful blast. the fall, the rush, I feel it, my body begins to change, my muscles expand, my sight becomes sharper, my hearing become keener and peering down into the surrounding woods I see the being not unlike the dead on the field. This one is alive. My training takes over; dipping my head I dive towards the strange looking creature.

It crouches appearing to take aim at me pointing a large apparatus in my direction, I am a regimentarian and when fully morphed I attain a level of lightning fast reflexes, fully morphed I wait sensing the inevitable, that's it, the creature wants to blast me out of the sky with that thing, I keep to my flight path, one of collision with it, the white of its eyes are fixed at me, I flank my left twiggle and moving to the right a loud crack rings through the air as it whizzes past me, I land feet first on top of the creature; with force. I crouch on it and grab its wrists and locking them hard I twist them to the left disarming it. It's now unconscious. I notice some differences this being in particular, has to the rest. With danger abated I revert back to my normal state of being, my body back to normal size.

The creature's body is fragile. When I held its wrists I could feel its bone almost break, I had to hold back, for if I killed it who would answer the many questions I had. The being looked terrified of me, resembling the others but having more fur than the rest. Actually its fur seems to only exist on its skull. A loud silence ensues, so loud that I can hear the wind and the trees and the branches creaking. I must report this immediately, Just then I felt an acute pain on my left palm. Damn! It's not unconscious How did I miss that? Instinctively I jump back and up again, I see what appears to be a strange blinking object in my flesh, and pulling it out then throwing it away it explodes in the distance releasing a blue colored haze. Looking down I cannot sight it, the unconscious being is no longer there! This strange being is nowhere to be seen, it is not within my line of sight periphery or otherwise. Feeling the rush again I morph dipping my head releasing my twiggles in order to increase descent I touch down on the snow and assume a combative form, an open stance. Pushing the balls of my feet into the snowy floor below, my wound begins to heal, I raise both my hands saying "I fall by the power of twelve", my muscles begin to expand my eyesight become sharper, and my hearing becomes keen. Where is it? The apparatus is also nowhere to be seen. Almost immediately the thought crosses my mind. I hear the loud crack again this time the sound emanates from behind me, I twist to the left dipping my shoulders I rotate facing the direction of the blast, I push my left foot into the ground rotating my body I move in its direction I see it and follow, it drops the weapon trying to get out of sight evasively it moves through the thickly wooded area, I am hot on its heels. Where it goes I go, I am so close to it I can smell its fear, I swiftly pass through the blue fog from the object I threw away earlier, suddenly I feel nauseous instantly weak and with blurry vision, damn that must be some type of poison. It got me. My vision blurry I stagger and hit the snowy floor.

Strangers

I see my father practicing his katas outside, the grass is green but it is cold, I so loved watching him train, I watched him as he sliced through the air left and right, and ended up performing a sword stand, he was very agile and quick on his feet. He died when I was still a cubling, so I knew that I was dreaming, he looked at me and while upside down still in that sword stand position with his feet dangling above him perfectly balanced, he flashed a smile at me.

I jump out of the dream; I closed my eyes and willed myself out of it.

My eyes are heavy, I feel as if my brain has been put to a metal grinder and was then washed by rusty shrapnel. I can't think complete thoughts, I try to move my arm but I can't, I realize that my hands and legs are bound.

I see two much distorted shapes approach. I shut my eyes masquerading unconsciousness. They speak a strange nasal sounding language I could not understand. One of them came closer it pressed something attached to my leg and I instantly felt a shudder run through my system a kind of electrical shock. My eyes fully open, the one with all the fur on its head appears the one that escaped me earlier. It speaks to my amazement in my language it says to me, "you are much better than we anticipated; your readings are truly off the scales. It went on to say "we are from a far away corner of the universe **a place known as Ether**".

It said that they were sent here by the leadership on their home planet and that they represented a species that spawned my creator, they said his name was Dr Ling, "so you too have male and female species like us" I said; it said "yes we do" "that in time you will be able to differentiate us", I guessed it was male, he went on to say that Dr Ling empowered our twelve, that he was our grand architect, the one that gave my kind life. I could not comprehend what the creature was saying. I thought, My Creator, an architect? This has to be a joke.

I asked them what my creators name meant, because on Gruce, my world, our names have meanings, and usually the names are significant towards the life of its bearer. He said the architect of my kind indeed had a special name with a special meaning; his full name was Earth Ling. His name means productive soil, he was a geneticist, and its significance was that soil is synonymous with life, from it life comes and to it life goes. Earth is the constant transformer of energy, from life to life. And so Dr Ling had become the creator of so many forms of life on Ether.

He went on to explain the dead on my land saying that they arrived here by singularporation "a technology stolen from a race known as the Unspoken, with whom they were engaged in all-out war against.it said that they were here seeking my help. They have been monitoring our planet and others for a while now and they know our combative potential.

"Your twelve up until their demise several centuries ago were secretly keeping us abreast of the situation here on gruce."

I thought demise, what demise, the twelve are eternal. I let them carry on.

"We created you; millennia ago, probes were launched, sending them throughout the known universe from our quadrant. It was said that Ling was an esoteric thinker and from his secret research obtained coordinates to various location in deep space, Dr Ling was a trusted scientist and he had many powerful followers within the world government, they believed him even though he hadn't evidence to support his theory which was that intelligent life existed in other parts of the universe. Dr Ling after many years received a ping from this planet, the probes were programmed to ping once life giving substances had been confirmed, water, oxygen etc. but on Gruce there wasn't only water and oxygen present there were also forms of plant, animal and significant levels of atmosphere, gravity and so forth, sufficient for our kind to survive on it, Upon further inspection we found no evidence of real intelligence on it, there were no structures or anything here". Due to the immense distance between our two planets being close to 30 earth years apart, he sent a team of scientists and others on a one way trip to your planet, with his Creation, what he termed the game changer gene or the supergene, long story short it was spliced with the cells of what they thought was the most intelligent animal on your planet, what looked like a small polar bear type creature, the cell was then grown through Dr Ling's top secret cloning process, the super gene was a smorgasbord of DNA, the idea was to create an animal that would be intelligent and also lethal in the theater of combat, his creation would have military applications. The super gene comprised of DNA of other life forms from ether such as the raptor for its hunting and survival instinct and the dragon for its intelligence and flying capabilities. Most of you have the benign polar bear gene but less than 1% of your populace is affected by the phosis, giving those that have it the ability to morph and gain strength, acute senses, speed, flexibility, thermo vision, denser bone structure and the power of self-flight."

"We are the ones that gave you all your abilities.

"Dr Ling wrote a paper, that many considered baseless on his beliefs that humans were also engineered, he thought that the human race were the only anomaly on ether being that humans really served no purpose within the ecosystem. Humans were literally simply consumer's, who just used ethers resources without thought to the impact their actions would cause to the planets ecosystem. It is a general belief that He had secret evidence that led him to believe we humans were also created. He was given the benefit of the doubt due to the respect he garnered for his immense contribution to ether in other ways".

"We need you to speak to your great council on our behalf, those whom you call "Twelve". They would listen to you and advise you. We want you to convince them on our behalf to allow a few of your brothers to come through the singularity with us to help us defend our world.

"We have lost sixteen of our brave cybers on our mission here, a small sacrifice compared to the hundreds of millions of us that could be saved eventually if we work together. We have worked out all the issues in the device the singularity now works perfectly well. I asked him what a singularity machine was; he said it is a device that creates a star then collapses it thereby creating a rip in the time fabric or the space continuum enabling us to travel long distances though it from point to point in an almost instantaneous manner. If we came to your planet by conventional means it would take us thirty years to get here and by then ether would be no more.

Just as its story was getting interesting another one of their kind burst into the hall. This one looked quite different. It was completely furless and more defined than the others it was taller and very dark in complexion. As it walked in the being that had been talking to me referred to it as Sergeant Blade, I still wondered how I, understood everything they were saying.

Sergeant Blade approached me first pulling out what looked to me like long flexible looking needles from the base of my head which I never even noticed were there in the first place. Blade then looked at me holding the three needles in his furless palms saying now you know why you understand our language. "We uploaded it into your memory banks on a subconscious level". I told it to remove my restraints now; I understood then that they were not hostile if they were I would have been in a worse off position. It looked at another as if to get the order. The one it looked at nodded and in a few seconds the restraints were off. They told me that they would give me twenty four hours to talk to the Twelve. I would be their go between. They gave me a communication devise which I was asked to wear around my neck. It was slim and concealed underneath my fur. I was told to plead to the council on their behalf and if need be I was asked to arrange a meeting between them and the Twelve. Then they told me that they would wait for my return.

I walked out of the hall in a kind of daze. Strange things are happening but that's not the crazy thing - the crazy thing was the pace at which all these things are happening.

Twelve

My twiggles unfurled and I was airborne due east, towards the Temple of Light where twelve reside. It is a beautiful temple built atop what we call the Mount of Enlightenment. It rises into the clouds. We are a proud species grounded in many traditions and beliefs, it is said that those who reside within the Temple are twelve beings of light that are in tune with the universe through the mystical elements that surround the mountain, the waters, the trees, the earth, and the wind essentially the essence of our world. The council consists of twelve masters no more and no less. It was told to me by my father that the twelve are in a state of perpetual meditation; they need not eat, drink or sleep. We were told that once ages ago they were mortal and indeed physically taught outside the temple all over the different parts of Gruce, including Arbonan the forbidden zone, but one by one they all eventually ascended to immortality within the temple as masters who would guide and advise our leaders throughout the ages. As I glide towards the temple my mind is filled with all kinds of questions, why the visitors are at my home and why they chose me.

Approaching the crystal glimmering gates of the temple they slowly open just enough for me to fly through, the gatekeepers in their dark brooding way do not even care to watch me. I approach the front door of the temple and it is filled with such serenity so bright. As I enter the light seems to envelope me, I hear a faint hum, it emanates from the communication devise I was given, it goes on for a few seconds and then stops, I feel a slight tingle throughout my body and my twiggles retract, I begin to float free feet from the floor, I have no control as to which direction I float, I feel weightless, the power of twelve must be strong in here, I am being pulled by some force towards the hall of enlightenment. I am without control of my movement I recite the mantra, I fall by the power of Twelve'. I am drawn by the light and find myself before twelve orbs of intense lights of varying color the central orb floated towards me and then, The hum emanating from the communicator earlier began again but this time it was in a sequence of hums that went on for a few seconds and stopped, and it emanated from the orb now in front of me, A projection appeared from it, very much looking like the strange beings I had encountered on my land as if manifested of light, it spoke.

"Draemen you are of the oldest bloodline on Gruce and we have chosen you to form the first expeditionary force from Gruce, it will be a force of four. You and three others will go to the third planet from the sun within the Orion constellation. It is a home to hundreds of millions of intelligent inhabitants. They face an event of great challenge we are sending you and three other regimentarians to help them. Their survival will depend on you four. Draemen son of Marcsor the wielder, we know of your encounter with the visitors; and you will be blessed with further enlightenment in time, but now take with you this knowledge as you leave this temple, you are destined to unite and lead your three brethren at arms to the home planet of the visitors, and save them from their aggressors, now go and assemble the other three". I wanted to ask him why he looked like the visitors, the shape of his head his hands his legs etc, and how they chose me and how they knew of my residence but I didn't. I couldn't move I just floated in an embryonic state in front of this celestial projection.

With the Twelve we were told never to debate, just listen don't say a word just digest, we were told only to contemplate on the wisdom they imparted to us, I was given three names, Trool, Teak and Nenveve, they were to be the members of my team.

As I left the hall I was filled with a kind of quiet resolve, one that I had never felt before. The Twelve, by not mentioning the story about the Architect to me confirmed that those beings from Orion constellation were truthful with their story.

I thought I must contact the visitors and give them some sort of progress report; the wind brushed my furry face as I continued west towards home.

My mind was like a jumbled mass of information I had too many questions, I felt in the last few hours my life has been transformed into a fantastic tale, one I hadn't inkling as to how it would end. I just knew I had a huge role to play in a big story, and by the Twelve I shall do my best to play my part honorably in this unfolding series of events.

I approached my home and from above I saw that Sergeant Blade and the other two beings appeared to have been expecting me, as I touched down they approached.

Sergeant blade told the long furred one to take the metta data device from me the one with the long fur on its hair came up to me and gently removed the device from my neck it had a concerned look on its furless face, I told it I thought it was a communicator, instead of answering me, it looked at me dead in my eyes, its eyes were deep blue and I could sense a softness flowing from them. This one seemed to be more concerned than the other two. It asked me in a low and slightly shaky voice "how did it go?" to which I answered "very well." I briefed them on what happened, the sergeant asked me when the others would arrive; he reiterated that they were running out of time. I told him that I would have to locate them and give them their orders. He then asked me who they were, to which I answered, "they are the best of us". They were regimentarians like me.

I told the furless dark one that the regemetarians represent the best of us, our warrior class; there are differences that set us apart from normal Gruce, and these differences are noticed from birth. From infancy we are taken with our mothers to a place called the Foundation, and there we are put through many rigorous tests, mental as well as physical.

We are sent to the academy when we are of age, there we are taught the histories of our class and among other things: the way of phosis and how to gain control of and harness the five senses and all the combative forces including evasive flight.

A team of four is a very strong force. The long furred one said "Strong! How can a team of four match up to the Shadow Reapers?", to which I asked who are the shadow reapers, it then said they are the enemy, they deploy several companies of troops in every region they intend to colonize and in some cases thousands of troops are deployed in certain well defended areas. They have no emotion no fear they fight and fight till the last of their kind stands.

I told them that once I assembled the others, we would do all that was necessary within our abilities to help.

"Our land is vast and regimentarians are posted along its various boundaries, we are spread out in this way for defensive purposes only. Our threats have been from the sea 'I will need time to track down the other three Gruce."

I must find the three Teek, Nenveve, and Trool. Our land is divided into quadrants, the northern, western, eastern, and southern quadrants. The regimentarians are posted in order to protect the boundaries of the four. Our planet is water, and one big mass of land in between.

Our planet is mostly cold due to the fact that the sun sits so far away from us; it almost always snows, here on our land.

Trool

I went to the club house in the city and spent some time looking through the regimentarian posting rosters, and I found where the three regimentarians I was to locate were posted.

Shortly after, I went back home, geared up and then began my quest for the three. I headed north where I found out Trool was now stationed. He was an adrenaline junky I'm sure that's why he chose to be posted there, the northern most part of Gruce was frequently attacked by grubbers and he loved action. This Gruce was gallant and a hardened battle tested one. Trool had excelled at the academy; he was poetry in motion, a brutal fighter, and a perfect harbinger of the phosis.

Last I saw Trool was over four cycles ago, we did a course in abstract flight together in which I had gotten the highest score.

At the academy Trool was what we called "a born to fight"; we called him that because he had a near natural grasp of the regimentarian battle applications. He understood what was taught us in academy long before he ever gained admission.

There are a few like him. His mother was a regimentarian so while he was at the foundation during those formative years she had given him a head start in the knowledge of violence.

At the academy, when he was of age, we would be paired with each other for combat training but instead of one sparring partner he would be paired against three or four opponents. He was so fast the only time he actually lost was towards the end of the first cycle when he was challenged by our instructor Bussan. Bussan was a strong stout regimentarian, a no nonsense instructor who instructed us on unarmed combat he thought that aside from a lesson in combat Trool also needed a lesson in humility and caution.

The instructor morphed and using the one power channeled from twelve, attacked and paralyzed Trool using a technique he called transference, he left him to stew in his own pot of pain for a time. Bussan told him force is important but strategy and planning is too, with the right tactics you can take a less powerful force to victory against a more powerful foe, he said, "Trool, you must use your mind, for even in combat it is the most powerful muscle you have!" trool stood up when the effects of the attack had worn off, he told Bussan that he believed he was ready for another lesson, Bussan attacked the same way he did before, he morphed, but this time Trool blocked subtle but numerous attacks, and then he too morphed and reversed the transference maneuver back on Bussan, stunned for a second, Bussan used his inner chi to deflect the energy coursing through him to the ground below, and thus recovered quicker than trool did, earlier, he then smiled at trool and said for every attack there is a counter attack "your learning has truly begun". Bussan took Trool as his personal student and molded him into the complete warrior he now is today, an unbeatable force.

Trool now stationed in the northern most region of our land, a vast land full of agricultural and and gruce resources. This part we call Grubstone, its inhabitants are predominantly farmers. The regimentarians are stationed there in order to protect the pipe lines and the Gruce that control the piping stations. Our land is mostly cold, icy and snowy, but the soil of Grubstone has unique qualities, it is very fertile, we pipe sea water through the station to vast farm lands near the sea. The piping stations are gruced by stone melters smelting Grubstones by fire. Constantly the seawater is piped through the molten stones and thus heated, the water is pressured pumped through to the farm lands and piping systems all through the land. Thousands of pipes under the soil heat up the land and keeps the frost and surges of ice away so that through all the seasons the grounds remain fertile.

The Grubbers are creatures of the sea who through past cycles have developed an appetite for Gruce, they are the only sea creatures that actually breathe on land like us and can spend hours at a time on land. They are large in size, and are also the only sea creatures with legs sufficient to carry their weight on land. They move on land comfortably but due to their immense size their movement is very slow but they move with conviction and strength. The only forces able to stop them are the regimentarians. In the academy we ran many simulations on Grubber attacks, these were based on legendary battles fought against them in the past. Our predecessors documented information from many encounters. Those encounters form the basis of our simulations at academy; we have since known of their weaknesses. They seldom attack anymore. It has been many cycles since their last attack.

I approach Grubstone. I know this because huge bellows of steam can be seen coming from what appear to be the piping stations, they stretch for miles along the beaches, as far as the eyes can see. The snowy landscape is suddenly transformed to visions of greens, yellows, reds and blues, the famous Grubstone farmlands that stretch for miles and miles providing Gruce with all kinds of produce. From up here Gruce are seen farming them to efficient purpose. The sight is awe-inspiring; it's been a long time since I ventured here.

The regiment where Trool should be stationed is near. There it was, the landing zone, regimentarians are below, I begin my formation flight, a series of loops and dives, this is done so that the troops below see me and recognize my flight pattern. It's like a pass code, this way they would permit my landing without incident. My twiggles umbrella out and I begin my descent. I land on the demarcated spot. It actually feels good; the ground isn't cold for a change I am used to landing on cold snowy floors. A familiar face approaches,

"Draemen is that you? I knew that flying style was familiar, you were always the best flyer weren't you?"

"Creeto, you haven't changed a bit," I exclaimed. "Listen I am here on a confidential mission from Twelve, I was asked to locate Trool, he is still stationed here, right?"

"Yes he is, but first things first you must be famished, let us eat at my dwelling, I am sure in the west you Gruce don't eat like we do."

I am actually hungry, but the excitement of my mission has made me less so. Creeto tells me he will have his Gruce locate Trool and bring him to his home where we shall all dine together.

We take off for about a minute, a short flight. It was more like an elaborate jump and glide what we call a long jump, your twiggle need not fully unfurl for it. We land at his doorstep. we enter and he tells me that I go to the spare room. He sent me clean garbs and cleansing gel. They have an abundance of water in Grubstone and advanced water technologies so there bathing rooms are elaborate. Each dwelling has special piping systems that pump water into bathing modules through nozzles above your head and all around you. I disrobe and enter the bathing module. It closes. I toggle the water channels and a rush of hot water rains down on and all around me. It feels wonderful. We hardly see water not to mention heated water to bathe with back west.

I see the utensils arranged in front of me in the module. Creeto's helper hands me the gel through an opening overhead and leaves, I apply the cool gel and comb it through my fur making sure it's in every nook and cranny then I comb it through as the steaming water rushes through my fur. The gel foams and it slowly washes away very soothingly in a few minutes. I am through, the module shuts and the dryers come on, the air rushes through the same nozzles, it cools and dries me down. Once dried the module opens and I walk out dry and clean I put on the fresh garb laid out in front of me. Dressed and heading for the table I hear clattering of plates and laughter the sound of two Gruce conversing over a meal, appearing I see them that I expected, its Creeto and Trool. They both stand Trool comes close leaps towards me with a warm embrace, he looks really happy to see me; we sit and he dishes me food, the aroma is mouth-watering, I tell them how lucky they are to eat fresh produce every day. The dish is famous in Grubstone called vita mix and kraw soup, it's very tasty. After the meal I politely request that Creeto give me room to speak with Trool. When he leaves I run Trool through the recent events I had witnessed, and tell him what the Twelve agreed on.

He is so elated at their decision, he told me that at Grubstone it hasn't been at all what he expected it would be; the place had no action, so he was glad that we were chosen to honor our race. Trool is a born to fight and I understood what he was saying, he relishes any opportunity to use his talent. I could see Trool was truly elated at this opportunity, just as I had hoped he would be. With him by my side I know the Shadow Reapers will find it very difficult to prevail,

Suddenly a loud siren rings; "by Twelve!", he said with a huge grin on his face!

"We are under attack; it must be the Grubbers".

I ran back to the room and quickly wore the garb I had just changed from, my regimentarian uniform. It's been so long since I have seen regimentarians in the air on a formation attack.

"What are you waiting for Draemen? Let's join them'" Trool said, I excel in Flight so I quickly jumped, my twiggle unfurled and I was with them, Trool by my side. We flew towards the piping station now under attack, as we approach I can see four Grubbers of immense size wreaking havoc on the station below, with their every laborious step they destroy, the station is ablaze with red fire, the many Gruce operating the station are at risk. In every station there is always a regimentarian stationed there. We can see him engaging one of the smaller Grubbers.

In unison we all recite the mantra, "I fall by the power of Twelve,".

My sight becomes clearer my hearing keener I feel bigger and stronger than I ever felt before, I look at Trool, and he smiles and says

"You know we are bigger in Grubstone - faster and sharper right".

I agreed I do feel a difference, he told me it's the roid biotins we put in the vita mix.

"It makes us stronger, he said."Let me show you,"

Trool swooped down to the largest Grubber landing with force in front of it.

"Tt's called a power landing Draemen", he shouted, just after he created a small crater in the ground. The shock wave generated by his landing pushes the Grubber back a few meters, his twiggles revert, Trool claps his hands together steps a foot back and twists forward his twiggles sprout and he spins like a drill and energizes; the centrifugal force of his spin creates electrical energy, it can be seen around him from up here blue sparks around his body, his twiggles unfurl he flaps them hard pushing hard and fast backwards this pushes him hard and with force feet first he drills right through the Grubber. As he appears through the other side the creature growls loudly and fiercely, it would be its last. Upon hearing the final cry of the downed grubber the other three smaller grubbers make their way towards the beach attempting to escape the other regimentarians. I follow them, shortly I too am in the fray joining one of the groups, the Grubbers were no challenge at all for us once morphed we are hard to kill.

There is one Grubber left I leap and lifting my right leg up in an axe type motion I bring it down from an immense height following it down the head of the beast and through its face. It is down.

These things are no challenge, they are not thinking creatures they are only doing creatures, impulsive things.

The sun is setting and reconstruction of the station has begun. Regimentarians still morphed help the lesser Gruce, the workers assemble materials as they begin reconstruction, the molten Grubstone that spewed all over the grounds of the station is beginning to harden. Steam bellows from all over the grounds, fortunately the Grubbers move very slow so that afforded the workers the time to get out of the piping station before they arrived, there were no casualties recorded, it was a good day for the regimentarians.

I have since reverted to my normal state when Trool meets up with me, as it's getting late he says we better head to his home. Trool lives away from the regiment, he stays off camp near the watch post at the beach, as we approach I notice he lives a simple modest life, his dwelling is smaller than Creetos, and I see no piping around his abode.

"Trool why do you live this way"? A regimentarian of your status should have less humble dwelling, and piping at least." He smiles and says he does not like distractions that comfort brings. He said there was serenity on the beach that he loved, that it gave him time to train and time to meditate on more meaningful things. There was no piping I told him that I needed to wash the Grubber stench off me, and asked him where I would go, he said "to the beach my friend" and to that statement I told him that Creeto was a much better host than he was, "to the marvelous beach you say", I repeat sarcastically, he hands me a packet of gel and I set off for the beach which wasn't far at all, only a twenty second walk away.

The ebb and flow of the water serenades' the night like a sweet drum beating in synch with my heart. In the west we aren't permitted to go to the actual shores. It is outlawed not because of dangerous creatures but because the waters due east are hazardous to our health, this is due to its high sulphur content. Water is imported to the west from Grubstone. Hearing the faint hum of the pumping engines in the distance, I realize I am a world away from my farm, and with that thought I actually face the realization that I would soon be literally a world away at Ether, I wonder how its waters are. Are they clean like waters from this quadrant?

While I bathed in the freezing cold water I reminisce on the academy, there too the water was always cold, I remembered how Trool was so exceptional and how I expected his circumstances at the stage to be quite different than they were. I guess he took the lesson Bussan taught him to heart, today Trool looks less restless, still very confident but humble at the same time. He finally understood that arrogance can hurt you.

Nenveve

Trool had told me that Nenveve was at the northern outpost, a fairly inhospitable area this was the coldest region and furthest away from the rest of Gruce. gliding through the clouds. I could see the sun on my left in the horizon. I had a slightly offsetting feeling it was as if I was trying to outrun time but no matter how far I flew it was still there staring back at me like some sort of bright blinding judge.

After my cold shower the night before, I went in and saw Trool already asleep, we had a long day and I knew he deserved it so I let him be. But In the back of my mind I knew that there would soon be even longer days ahead. By the time I awoke the next morning Trool was preparing for his duties. We met over some hot breakfast. Trool gave me a gift of some roots, he said they would boost my energy whenever I needed a push, I told trool to join me in 72 hours the next three days at my farm, and I was off heading north to the outpost known as Arbonan where I would locate Nenveve. I began my journey early so I could get the message across in time. Nenveve was actually a female Gruce and regimentarian.

Arbonan was the location for the headquarters of regimentarian special operations. Most things that went on there were highly classified and on a need-to-know basis within the regimentarian corps. It was said to be the location where most of our classified programs took place and only regimentarians who excelled in psycomatics were posted there in order to train with the moon worshippers. They would be taught to harness their abilities in order to gain their full potential, it was said that these abilities included, remote viewing, and the art of knowledge without knowing and twigless flight.

when I was at the foundation before academy I really did not know Nenveve on a personal basis, I would see her but I always kept my distance, sometimes we would meet, usually exchange smiles and greeting, Nenveve was an ace in games and tactics, her scores were consistently record-breaking. Games and tactics was an aspect of the regimentarian training that dealt with the power of thought, the premise was that, there is power in knowledge and with knowledge at least half of any challenge is overcome.

She had the ability to meld her mind with other intelligent life, this enabled her to know what their thoughts were at any time, and in some cases this power also allowed her to control the minds of her opponents by bending theirs to her will.

As youths in the foundation, we all underwent initial tests in strength, and knowledge but we were also tested in psycomatics, and depending on how well we performed in any aspect of training we were presented we would be assigned areas of concentration, I was a great flyer so I was made to concentrate on flight, I was one of the best.

It was said that Neneveve's score in psycomatics was off the charts that made her top of her group. She was gifted she could sense fear, pain, and most of all she could tell if ones heart was truthful or the opposite. I was told by a friend when in training that she would often change her personality and actually become her opponent, in essence know what the regimentarian cadet would do before he or she did it. In fact, shortly after we were enrolled in academy there was a rumor that she could not only transform her personality but she could also transform her appearance that she could shape shift, although I had never seen her do this. We were told that some within the regiment in the past were said to have had the ability to morph beyond the fall.

Nenveve used her skill to become the best at games and tactics. She always had the best solutions to any problems thrown at her. This is why she was posted to Arbonan the forbidden land, after the academy.

I never was so close to her but her story was well known by all of us who were in the academy at the time.

As I glide through the clouds, I realize that I didn't really know her, I never took the time to, not because I couldn't have but actually because I avoided her. Back then I was averse to mingling with psycomats who due to an accident in their genealogy could know my hidden truths and dreams.

The temperature was beginning to drop drastically as I was approaching Arbonan, my twiggles felt heavier; ice was beginning to form on them. It was quite a desolate area few Gruce ever ventured there and fewer lived there. It was like a desert of snow and ice, the population there was insignificant, Arbonan was a large indoor base that comprised of about a thousand Gruce, regimentarians and moon worshippers and the latter of whom I had never set eyes upon.

At the camp psychomats were all over.

I had been gliding through the air for quite a time close to twelve hours and the shiny dome upon the camps very high walls could be seen. The bright Arbonan lights beamed through windows of the structure. I could see the landing zone some distance away and the circular landing lights. The sun was setting. I began my formation flights from the regulation height and desistance so that the regimentarians below recognize me as they did at the Grubstone base.

All of a sudden I felt a similar feeling I had felt when in the temple of light, I felt warm and relaxed, my twiggles retracted by themselves but I was still floating in the air, I was being controlled by another force, I was surrounded by a warm cushion of pure force, my descent was ever so slow and gradual, It was as if I was being brought down lovingly, as soon as my feet touched the snow covered landing zone I regained control of my body that force was no longer in control.

I was in the center of some Gruce in translucent hooded light material their garb was form fitting, the Gruce were bearing flaming torches their heads all bowed slightly, I could only see their furry chins, these I knew weren't regimentarians. They looked sculpted and extremely fit as if within their normal state, they were as fit as if they had morphed.

I was told by one of them in a very muffled but stern voice to follow, which I did. The Arbonan camp is domed it is quite large it was constructed this way because of the harsh weather of the region. I noticed that the one marching in front of us was actually floating, he waived his hand and the gate opened. As we followed him, without turning round to face the gate, he waved his hand behind him and the gate closed. I guessed that they were all psycomats, but not regimentarians, they must be moon worshippers.

As we walked on I noticed some very strange things, I noticed regimentarians floating around feet of the floor without unfurling their twiggles. Soon the other psycomats behind me left and the one in front led me to an office, as he opened the door, I saw Nenveve, she looks so different now I was in awe of her, her fur was gleaming by the fire light, her eyes were deep and blue as if an ocean laid within them. She looked absolutely stunning. She greeted me by my name.

"Draemen," she called, "it's been an age since I last saw you!"

"I believe we were at foundation together, weren't we?" to that I said yes, and I told her that I was sure she knew why I came, that by now she must have melded with me.

She stood up I noticed she was not touching the floor, I found it so interesting that every Gruce I had seen thus far had apparently been floating. she looked at me and smiled she knew what I was thinking, she went on to answer the question I had wanted to ask, I felt a little violated as if I was weak and due to that fact, she would take advantage of me.

Nenveve said this is the reason Arbonan is so remote and situated so far away from the rest of Gruce many would not understand why we few have such gifts, it would be scary for most of them, so we live here with the moon worshippers in harmony so that we can benefit from one another, the moon worshippers are natural psycomats, they were taught by their order to hone their talents from birth.

"I am among two hundred Gruce here at present we are the cream of the psycomats within the core, we train with the moon worshippers and they give us insight as to the best and most efficient ways in which to use our gifts. We regimentarians have through generations learnt to harness the military applications of our gift, and the moon worshippers have harnessed mostly the spiritual aspects of it."

The moon worshippers have learnt what to eat and what not too, in order to realize their full potential. I brought out the energy boosting roots that Trool gave me, Nenveve noticed them, and she termed them zeng roots. She said I should get rid of them, I asked why and she said that they grew stronger things here. She told me about something they have developed, "it's a hybrid of many plants, this is available for use by regimentarians only, we call it the blue lotus, it allows for non psycomats to temporarily evolve from thier normal Gruce state into a psycomatic one; with this root a regimentarian can for a period of time become a psycomat of beginner stage, where he or she can enjoy a few of our basic abilities. For example you will be able to perceive thoughts of the enemy, and with enough concentration meld with them. As of yet it hasn't been tested on non psycomats."

I returned the zeng root to my pouch.

She told me to rest, wash and eat; tomorrow she would take me through things I would need to know, in preparation for the mission the Twelve had set us upon. I did feel hungry and a bit weak. The mind meld she earlier performed took a lot out of me; she said my room was on the higher levels at about the sixtieth floor, she said these are where the dwelling units were located.

As we stepped out of the hall I noticed there weren't elevators, back east, we have elevators in the taller buildings, because they don't allow the use of twiggles indoors. Nenveve handed me a small pill she told me to ingest, after which I should follow. She then floated above me towards the dwelling floors, I put the pill in my mouth and swallowed, I instantly felt warmer, immediately understanding why the moon worshippers I met earlier were wearing hooded gowns of light material not adequate to keep warm in the sub frozen landing zone, I guessed their geneology made them warmer. The pill she gave me was luminescent kind of turquoise blue, I thought this must be the blue lotus she spoke of, in an instant I felt warmer and lighter in weight, I looked down and realized my feet were no longer on the floor. I looked up and imagined I was following Nenveve, my body was so relaxed my twiggles didn't sprout, I began to rise and shortly I was with her in the air moving closer to the enormous beautiful domed ceiling. it was quite amazing, a gigantic Muriel of a regimentarian and moon worshipper walking together on an icy path, all of a sudden I heard a voice quite whispy and full of echoe say to me, "it's nice to fly without your twiggles for a change isn't it" Nenveve turned and looked at me this time she said "don't worry Draemen it's me Nenveve you are now for the time being one of us and you are therefore open to the meld that was my voice in your thoughts, it's not to clear now but it will get clearer, now your mind is melded with mine".

She landed on the sixtieth platform, the floor where my quarters were. She walked me to the door of my unit, and said we would meet by morning. She handed me another pill a bright yellow one she told me I was to take that one when I woke in the morning. She informed me libations will be brought to me.

I walked in. It was a fairly cozy room quite warm, and sweetly fragrant. I disrobed and continued to the bathing room, there it was, the module again but this one was not as

44

fanciful as the one at Creetos's place. I jumped in, and closed it awaiting the lovely experience I had at Creeto's. There was a rush of water but it was warm, not as hot as the waters of Grubstone. The experience was over in a few minutes and I felt good. As I came out I saw an amazing spread laid out before me, all types of food, uplings, dalas, tators, and cued tac, apparently I also learned that in Arbonan there are also livestock farmers, as I dug in, I noticed that the meat was so well baked, the vegetables were scrumptious and crunchy not overcooked and I love the mixture of spices, the tac was super flavorful. I ate to my satisfaction. They also brought up a jar of honey wine with the meal, I immediately remembered the rgementarians and moon worshippers aren't supposed to drink, then that voice again, it says "it's Nenveve, forgive my intrusion", I am still melded with you and have been enjoying your thoughts since I left you, I must also take the opportunity to apologize about the not-so-hot water, now as for the drink, her voice went on, "the regimentarian constitution states under the section 54 prohibition that the regimentarian must not drink while on duty, and as you know we are always on duty, this in essence means that we are forbidden from alcohol drink of any kind, but we psycomats have the ability to alter our state of mind at will and because we are capable of such control the psycomats are permitted under the constitution to drink what they wish, therefore you can drink the honey wine it is necessary for you it will awaken something precious in your spirit."

With that last whisper in my mind the voice was gone. I all but jumped into the wine, it was so sweet and subtly intoxicating, I had to try the meld on my own, I looked inwardly at myself and I felt my furs stand and I actually felt my body begin to rise I was floating. As I focused on Nenveve, I felt my body come back down, I spoke through my mind from within I made a simple comment,

"This drink is fascinating!"

I got no reply but I remained in concentration.

"Boo!!!!" my eyes immediately opened.

"Nenveve is that you?" I heard laughter then she said it was. she told me to get some rest, that we had a lot to cover tomorrow.

I lay down on the mat and slowly drifted into sleep.

The Craft

I awoke the next morning without my usual grogginess, I felt absolutely tip top energetic. I immediately put on my gear, "You may open your door'". It was her voice again.

I, not being conversant with the mind meld spoke out loud asking, "is that you?" to which the voice answered, "yes and my name is Nenveve not her voice, and during a mind meld you need not speak out loud that defeats the purpose of us melding", I answered still speaking out loud, "ok". She then told me to open my door, as I opened I saw a very dark Gruce in a maroon hooded garb. He lifted the hood and introduced himself.

I noticed his hood was a bit different. This one had a white line that began at the front of the hood and as he turned around saying I should follow I noticed the white line snaked all the way down in a perfect straight line through to the back. When he lifted the hood and introduced himself, he said his name was Bokoonan, I told him mine was Draemen, he then said, as we got to the platform, that I should take the yellow pill I was given. I reached into my pouch and found it, then I swallowed it, and almost immediately felt a most uncomfortable feeling, it was an internal one as if my muscles were being stretched, contracting in a subtle almost spasm like elastic way, there was no pain though. Bokoonan said that before heading to Nenveve we must wait for the pill to embed, he said my mind and body were being aligned this process is called embedding, in a minute or so your body will normalize.

Actually as he spoke I already felt the internal contractions lessen, it soon stopped but I didn't feel any improvement in me, "you will!". It was Nenveve's voice this time, her voice sounded like her voice there was no more echo it was as clear as if she was right here speaking to me.

"Bokoonan will bring you to me."

He stood at the edge of the platform and he dove off it I watched him freefall all the way appearing as if he would hit the floor below but thankfully I guessed they stopped him only a few feet from the floor, as if he was caught by something. In my mind I thought he was caught the same way I was when I approached the landing zone and I surrender all control. I believed I would be caught by the same force too, with faith in the psycomats of Arbonan I took the plunge and dropped off the edge my velocity increasing the gravitational forces had affected my eyes, I always felt that free fall speed was the fastest speed we achieve.

"It is not!" Nenveve voice again.

"I will guide you. Breathe in and when you are ready exhale all the air in your lungs and you will stop."

"You mean you aren't the ones who are going to stop me?" the floor was fast approaching I exhaled out and I basically willed myself to stop and I did.

"Well done Draemen, you have passed the first of a few tests."

I thought "test, what tests" I came here to give you your orders from the Twelve, I believe that supersedes any tests. She laughed. She said, "I was told of this mission over a month ago. I was contacted by the Twelve directly through the mind meld, you think you are here to give me information about a new event but you are actually here to be prepped for that mission, the one to the planet Ether."

"The very first test you took and passed very well I must say, in games and theory is called mind over matter. Your physical surrounding is no limitation to your abilities, your mental strength is your only limitation and asset, it gives you boundless limits, and after all did you ever think you could fly without your twiggles?"

There was a silence, I saw Bokoonan nod, he then told me Nenveve had given him the order to hurry me to her, I asked where we were going, and he grinned at the same time saying that Nenveve was waiting for us at the games hall. I thought she really means business I'm going to go through basic training all over again.

We got there, she was in black active dress, this was what we wore in the academy during training, I was handed one by another Gruce in the same garb as Bokoonan, I took it. I asked her what the white line on their hooded gowns meant, she said, "every cycle or so the moon worshippers select a few regimentarians to join their order and by our constitution we must agree to it, this act keeps us in synch with the moon worshippers and sort of ensures that we do not have any conflict against them, it solidifies our bond, sort of like marriage, those with the white lines on their gowns are actually regimentrians who were absorbed into the order of the moon worshippers. While in dome, they can wear this garb if they choose but on missions they must be fully geared up and fully outfitted in accordance with regimentarian regulation."

Bokoonan took me to the locker rooms where I could change into the formfitting light and comfortable training suit, I was changed and out within a short while.

I consciously tried to limit my thoughts, I felt naked here in Arbonan as if my mind was totally exposed and any one could pick from it.

"Why are you closing your mind?" Nenveve asked.

I answered out loud I said, "Because I don't give access to my inner most thoughts freely."

Nenveve also spoke out loud, "Arbonan is a sacred place and they the pysycomats had sworn an oath not to use their powers of perception to harm fellow regimentarians or Gruce or any innocent life form in any way.

She said they were honor bound to keep to the oath, she assured me that all my secrets were safe with her, that the only way I will be prepared now is to fully accept the training, and for it to work my mind needs to be open, I must be my honest self, that it would be for my own good. I agreed and decided to think freely now sharing my inner most thoughts with everyone in the hall. The hall was quite large it was about one thousand square meters, with walls ditches and all other forms of obstacles around, there were lots of objects positioned all over, some seemingly floating on their own and some positioned on the floor.

Nenveve told me that the series of pills she had been giving me were what they called pull ups, they are designed here at the Arbonan application labs, the pills are made for the regimentarian corps, they are necessary for embedding.

"You Draemen are the first of many regimentarians who will benefit from these pills. You will be the first regimentarian to be embedded.

"There are four pills in all each has its own process or function. The first one I gave you is an extract of the blue lotus plant in combination with some vita biotins and other strength enhancing roots, the first pill depending on what the taker can do after ingesting it, will determine how far he can proceed with the program. She said when I took the first one and was able to follow her up to the dwelling units on the sixtieth floor without sprouting my twiggles she knew I was a prime candidate for the pull up program. For our mission to succeed it would be necessary for our team to have psycomatic abilities, she went on saying that as a psycomat her training was basically mind oriented and hardly physical, but that I

Trool and Taek on the other hand have other expertise which are considered very valuable in the theater of combat, where we will soon be headed. She reinstated all our skills would be further enhanced by the pull up program, I as an avid flyer and combatant, Trool a born to fight and Taek an instructor at the academy.

I believed all our skills would be enhanced by the pull up program. Nenveve handed me a red pill next, "this is the second to the last of the pills; the first was to awaken the dormant part of your brain which enables forethought, telekinesis, and aero portation: this part of the brain is known as the third median".

That term was new to me.

"The second pill, the yellow one was designed to synch your body with your mind so that you would be freer and doubtless in your movement, as you make a thought your muscles would function absolutely in synch with your mind. It enhances the synaptic flow within your nervous system by growing millions of roots out of your nerves, in essence your muscles merge with your nerves, this makes you much faster and sensitive to your surroundings.

"I am sure you noticed the muscular structure of the moon worshippers in Arbonan and how they are seemingly immune to cold, this is because their musculature is so enhanced, they move faster and harder than any normal regimentarian.

"The more they train the more they burn fat and create muscle mass. You will soon notice the same effect on you too Draemen."

She handed me the third pill a red one and said I must take it before this final test.

I took it and began to feel as if time was slowing down. Every color became vivid. My sight was keen, my hearing amazing and I could hear a kind of ticking from one of the objects positioned on the floor about two hundred meters away, I could hear subtle humming sounds, it was amazing and I wondered what it was,

"Oh the humming you here is the sound of the thoughts of the moon worshippers about to make themselves present to you. Go to the center of this hall to meet them but I must warn you, you cannot morph, and if you do you would fail this most important test. They are waiting, go now"!

I made my way to the center of the hall. I felt my fur rise all over my body as instinct took over I thought "to fall by the power of Twelve.

Nenveve's voice now loud in my head **"Do not fall"**.

I stabilized my blood flow by power of thought, six worshippers in their hooded garb appeared, Bokoonan the only one with the white stripe floated in front of me, they all disrobed exposing the training suits similar to the one I was wearing. I felt myself become lighter. I was floating too. They surrounded me floating in a circle around me, I felt their thoughts they were all as one, their minds were in full synchronicity. I could hear their hearts beating absolutely in synch, in a second the tension was broken, Bokoonan was upside down his feet come at me with kicks directed at my face I anticipated and shifted to the left dodging them, I felt a sudden tingling sensation it must be the pull ups doing their work. I floated upwards as I did looking down only then realizing that I had just dodged all manner of attacks from the other five Gruce below. I was in tune with myself; the tingling I felt must have been some sort of remote sensing ability warning me of the impeding attack from the other regimentarians. This was no test this was full on combat, I only then realizes that Trool was truly amazing in the academy always taking on multiple attackers. I remembered what he told me then, he said that he saw his adversaries as inanimate objects to be moved as he saw fit out of his path or into it. I decided to trust in what he told me so long ago. Although I felt handicapped without morphing, without the fall, I engaged myself, falling into the combative stances instead for the first time without the fall. My mind was in synch with my body I attacked them, as they floated up towards me I blocked simultaneously striking them one by one with swift combinations of knife and hammer fists, blocking their individual attacks and hitting them hard. With each hit I felt whatever I had contact with break or fracture there were muffled crunches and cracks with my every strike. In a minute they were all down, Bokoonan was the only one still standing he yelled out the words I fall by the power of Twelve, "oh no!" I thought as he began to morph into the most ferocious looking regimentarian I had ever laid eyes upon, his twiggle span was longer than usual, he moved towards me so fast that it appeared as if he had been catapulted in my direction I was tempted to fall, but I didn't remembering what Nenveve said, this is a test after all, the pull ups I have taken down are definitely doing their work, he swung at my head, I ducked he immediately tried to engage me with strikes using his feet one after the other, I blocked them with my forearms, as they came, I felt nothing.

If a regimentarian once morphed hits you anywhere while you weren't morphed, I remembered, that part of your body which took the impact of the hit would break, this is why at academy we never fought an opponent who wasn't morphed while we were. He turned round trying to use his left leg in an axe motion targeting my shoulder blades, I moved to the left, he was exposed I gave him multiple hits with both arms to his neck region continuously till we were on the ground. I felt as if I was morphed, so much confidence so much speed and strength, I could feel he was distempered, unbalanced he blocked my last hammer fist, grabbing my right arm so I used my left instantly striking his hands away breaking the hold. I heard a crack, I had broken his right forearm, I was amazed because when fully morphed a regimentarians bones become very dense, he reversed his twiggles and flew backwards away from me almost as quickly as he had earlier flown towards me.

I followed him knowing he was trying to find some breathing space in order to enter a healing stance and heal his broken bones, I didn't give him the chance I couldn't believe what I had just accomplished, I beat a regementarian into retreat while he was fully morphed, an unheard of feat. Suddenly I heard the same ticking sounds I had earlier heard, it seemed to emanate from the objects positioned around the hall, I guess they weren't there for decoration I turned around and faced the one the ticking sounds closest to my position. My senses felt heightened. The ticking stopped. About a hundred sharp lethal looking projectiles shot out from it in my direction. I stood there and as they approached I waved my hands to the left and right successively in front of the objects creating a disturbance in air flow in front of them sufficient to divert them to the floor below, I heard some ticking again, my senses were so heightened I could actually hear the flaws in these machines, this time I knew what the ticking sounds meant, so I decided to nip the threats in the bud. I floated towards it this time it felt more like I flew towards it with my twiggles because I moved at great speed. I got there fast even faster than I would have using my twiggles, as I approached the object I engaged it with multiple strikes till it burst into bright flames, and all its internal mechanisms including unspent projectiles were now a hot mass and lay displayed, smoking on the floor below.

I decided to go even further, I went towards every device I saw in the hall it was so fast as if time stood still, it was as if once I thought of floating towards the object I actually appeared there. I destroyed them all with a combinations of strikes. As I did I saw Bokoonan again he was above me, he attacked diving towards me I moved to the right to dodge his attack and to my surprise he was nowhere to be seen, then I saw him beneath me. He flew towards my direction I moved to the right trying to dodge whatever attack he planned, and again Bokoonan was nowhere to be seen like he disappeared or something, I heard a kind of frustrated yell echoing from a distance it sounded like Bokoonans voice, I channeled my thoughts to his in order to meld with him, it worked I was in his mind. I invaded it so easily, I heard him say to himself the following words, "Draemen has achieve areoportation!"

In my head I thought, that explains it how I seemingly dodge his blows and don't see him and after a few seconds I do, because I teleport myself from one point in the hall to another trying to avoid or dodge Bokoonans attacks, I know now that I have mastered the telekinetic senses.

That also explains why I was able to reach the ticking objects so fast. I decided not to block his screaming attack anymore, I held my space, anticipating his attack and instead of blocking or dodging I flew into it using both hands in an outwards motion blocking both his arms hard, hearing them both break I hit the center of his chest cracking his sternum; the force of the strike sent him plummeting to the floor hard, and he lay there motionless.

I landed subtly inches from his body. I felt so warm and full of energy, I felt as if I could go on and on. I was not at all drained of energy the difference in me was so clear. As I made my way towards Nenveve, I took a deep breath and centered myself, I believed I could quiet my thoughts, I believed by thinking in whispers, I could stop her from melding with me. She was surrounded by about twenty Gruce they all held cleaning utensils - sweepers, packers and so on and they all nodded in unison and walked towards me, actually passing me they went toward the scene of the battle. They walked past me and started clearing all the debris from the training session, Nevevev looked at me and smiled, she told me that it was a success. The embedding had worked, that I have seamlessly adapted to the physiological effects of the pull ups; "you will now be given the final pill, the mecur pill!"

"This will embed the changes to your physiognomy into your system, without this in the next two hours you will lose all the new abilities you have gained, but once you take this pill your abilities shall be embedded in your system for a whole cycle. Will you like that Draemen"? She asked, and off course I said yes, the challenge that lay ahead of us would be more likely overcome with these abilities.

She gave me the pill, and told me that once I get to academy I must not let anyone know of my psycomat ability, that this program was a secret one, only the Twelve and very few high ranking pyscomats know. Then I take the pill as I do I put my hand in my pouch and pull out the root I was given by Trool back at Grubstone, I look at it for a moment and I actually consider throwing it away, but intuition tells me that I may need it sometime so I throw it back in my pouch.

Nenveve tells me that she would meet me once the rest of the team were assembled at the appointed location and that I should prepare mentally for what we were about to face. She said we were going to be in an old world an ancient one once known as earth and I should prepare for the unexpected.

In these past days I had seen so much change, both physical and psychological, I have been made privy to some mind shattering information, but thankfully I have been able to assimilate the information with no damage to my psyche. I feel so much stronger, quicker and more intelligent than ever before. I believe now more than ever that I can overcome whatever challenge the moons may lay before me.

Teak

I head back west towards Bambush. Though I now have the power to fly without twiggles, I do. I was cautioned not to expose the pull up program. Nenveve told me to be discrete with my new gifts while on Gruce, and not to let any Gruce outside the domed city of Arbonan know of it. I unfurl my twiggles and take to the skies. Gruce are ignorant to thinking outside their life station. We are a peaceful race.

The moons shone bright almost as bright as that faithful night at Scarfend, when I met the aliens from Ether. The faint hum of my twiggles permeated the silence of the night sky, I could see the lights of Bambush ahead. To the left I see the hill and the dark sea in front of it. On the right I see the gate of our great academy, the school where generations of regimentarians had been produced. I flank and head in that direction knowing that somewhere in that complex institution Teak lay in his bed without knowledge of what I am sure will come as a surprise to him.

I approach the academy gates, below, my twiggles umbrella out and I descend. This place brings back so many memories.

It is late now, but the sooner I make contact with Teak the better. I have the unsettling feeling that time was against me. I was told when I inquired about Teak many cycles ago, that he lectured at the academy, but I never did ask what subject he taught. I learnt that Teak was a fine regimentarian, after all he was of good stalk, in the sense that he was from a long line of Regimentarians. Normally it's only one family parent that has the gene, but in his case both his parents were regimentarians and they too were from a long line of similar stock. Like Nenveve, Teak was not a close friend at the academy, but like Nenveve his name preceded him, we all knew about his analytical skills, and his acute intellectual prowess. He was known for his robust knowledge of the history of regimentarianism, command, combat and tactics in the theater of war. I would have guessed that Teak would become a lecturer, in fact in academy he would occasionally correct our lecturers when they would make certain assertions he did not agree with or what he would refer to as minor distortions of reality.

"Halt who goes there", one of the guards exclaimed, to which I said "Regimentarian class 1 Draemen Turran son of Marcsor."

To which he reiterated "Friend or foe!"

I immediately said friend. In my head I wondered how anyone would respond "foe!" in that situation except for a moron. He then said you may approach to be recognized. I approached the guard and once he recognized my regimentarian glyphs, he told me to follow the path. As I walked through the gates, I felt as if I had been transported back in time to when I was new to this place - this house of pain, hardship, and great accomplishment. This path in the academy is a white path of marble stone, this is a walkway that only regimentarians may take, and it is known as the path of promise.

During my time as a cadet we would watch regimentarians walk on this path I walk on now, but back then as cadets we were not permitted to walk on it, we would only watch and hope that our time would come.

I followed the path to the administration hall. Where I would get the information I needed about Teak, and where to find him. As I approached the double doors of sapphire glass, I pondered on Teak, how he gave up the life of a fighting regimentarian, and opted instead for the life of a lecturer.

As I entered the hall, the first thing that hit me was a large portrait of the commandant of the academy, what surprised me more was who the commandant was. It was Teak, apparently somewhere between the time I discovered the aliens on my land and now, Teak had been elevated from the point of professorial to commandant of the entire academy, this must be some sort of record. He was barely older than I was and he is the commandant already, I thought that was amazing, but I knew he could not refuse this assignment no matter what position he had risen too. I met a cadet at the reception, and asked him where the commandant was, he told me to go east, that they were conducting fire light exercises with cycle five cadets. I asked him how Teak became commandant, he divulged that the outgoing one had passed away suddenly all but two days ago, and in the interest of continuity Teak was appointed commandant almost immediately after. Then I asked when he would be back and was told the exercise would be done by daybreak, so I would be accommodated till then. I decided I would leave a message for the commandant with him, for his ears only; I left it on the encrypted dat recorder system all level alpha regimentarians enjoy.

I left my message and on my way out I noticed young Gruce cadets begin to assemble at the parade grounds for morning physical training; not so long ago I was in their position, back then my eyes still sleepy but full of hope of the promising and fulfilling life in the regimentarian corps. I felt now more than ever before a feeling of resounding accomplishment, now I had an opportunity to make myself, my family, the regimentarian corps and our race proud. I was filled with the belief that what I was about to embark upon, was destiny's making, or some sort of karma. No matter what it was, I felt that I had the responsibility to play my part in this complex situation with the best of my abilities

As I approached the gate my mind was still adrift in thoughts when I suddenly realized that the few cadets on the grounds were staring at me, for a minute I thought it was because they rarely see us outsider regimentations walking the path, then I noticed what it was that caught their attention, I was gliding a few feet off the ground I immediately bent down to jump, my feet still off the ground coming up I made it appear as if I power jumped, in an instant launching myself quite high while simultaneously unfurling my twiggles I took to the sky. I wonder if I floated along the path long enough for them to be sure that I was actually floating, I hoped not.

I needed to get home I had been gone for some time now, and I quite missed my home the quaint woods the snow covered grass and the thick pink yellow bushes and the sweet smell of weh flowers from my door. I wondered if the aliens were still stationed at my home and I hoped that they kept well out of sight, I hoped they were there, because I had one or two questions on my mind.

It was daylight as I approached my land; I could see Scarfend to my right. That sweet taste of cloud In my mouth again, now with my land below me I begin my descent, my twiggles umbrella out as I came down, shortly my feet were on the ground.

Two of the beings approach with a concerned look on their faces, the darker one Sergeant Blade, asked me where the rest were, I told him they were on the way. I decided not to let them know about the pull up program, it would be my little secret. With a little concentration I was able to meld with the sergeant, It was too easy with little resistance I was in, first a rush a vivid stream of utter strangeness, outer worldly images of billions of these weak creatures slight differences in their sizes, shades. They all living and working on a seemingly very different plain of existence, I began seeing more clearly.

I could see Sergeant Blade in his youth and present, he was a warrior, his mind was full of death mostly, and that was what I saw. I also felt his immense pain as I dug deeper, images of those they called the unspoken, the Shadow Reapers appeared. They were gigantic but did not look threatening at all, there was a kind of light and softness an aura of benevolence about them, then the pain hit me like a power slam, I was filled with a kind of heartache, horrific images consumed me I saw that everywhere these giants went death would follow. Sargent Blade was of the marine core an elite fighting force specifically trained for combat.

I saw that he was engaged in an age old war before the unspoken arrived. A generation of combatants were engaged in an age old religious war, he was a warrior, one of the knights of the temple, and they fought against a group they called the army of mythra. Countless of their kind was killed, from the images I gathered from the meld, both groups at war looked the same, the only differences between them was their religious beliefs, it was mind boggling to me, because in my world, a Gruce can never kill a Gruce, probably only another creature, if the other creature presented a risk.

Billions had died from the old conflict. Then the unspoken arrived, and deployed the Shadow Reapers they came and almost immediately the army and the knights joined forces against a common threat. When this happened both groups placed their differences aside, in order to face a common enemy.

It was so vivid, I stopped the meld, and the sergeant did not have a clue of the information I had just acquired from him, my secret would remain thus.

Both strangers were quite anxious to know how long it would take before the other three Gruce would arrive. The strangers were quite well hidden there was no trace of the dead on my land, they had all been cleared.

We walked in and there it was the one that attacked me that night. In a second I was in, I melded with her, I felt so much warmth, I knew for sure this was a female of their species, she was also a warrior like Blade, but she fought for the other side, she fought for the army of mythra, taking part in that very bitter and age old conflict.

She was a capable fighter and well respected among her peers. I could feel that she was different, I could not see her more distant past, her childhood, her life seemingly began on the battle field, I also noticed that she was far more fascinated by me than the rest of them, probably because of my appearance and how different I looked. What I saw was her own account of the arrival which was slightly different than that of the sergeant.

I felt what she felt that night we met on the snow when we locked eyes just before she attempted to blast me out of the sky. It wasn't fear like I thought then, although in such a precarious situation the thought she had, were actually thoughts of concern for me, she was thinking about my wellbeing, and at the same time she was impressed by my capabilities. She must

have had information about my kind, from the meld I could see
that she was not in the least surprised at all by my appearance,
in fact she expected me, I had images of what appeared to be
her debrief, she and four others one of which I recognized
as one of those dead on my property. They appeared to be
part of a separate mission. There were pictures very unclear
ones, fragments, hazy images, in one of the pictures; I could
make out a Gruce-like figure. In the other picture there was
a fully morphed Gruce, twiggle unfurled and all, they were
being informed by the soldier giving them the debriefing but
I couldn't understand, it was as if her psyche was blocked, I
ended the meld, maybe she would better explain to me herself.

I wanted to get her full story for some reason I failed to
gain access from the meld. I needed to know more about their
world since they definitely knew a lot about mine. I believed
I could get all the information I needed from her voluntarily.
I looked at her hardened face, and noticed some tiny scars on
her left cheek as we locked eyes, I could tell there was no fear.
She noticed me staring and told me what the scars were, she
said that it was something she picked up during the arrival,
I pretended not to know of what arrival she refereed to, and
she answered the arrival of the unspoken ones. I then asked
what her name was and she told me to call her Staff Sergeant
Ayeesha bell.

As she said that the other being walked in, the one I saw
at the barn when I came too, suddenly understanding their
language, the one who appeared to give them orders, he didn't

speak much he just motioned his hand to me as if to say come with me or I should follow him. I did. We went behind my home by my tool shed where I saw a contraption, some kind of machine, with a platform. He asked me if I knew what it was and I told him I didn't, he then said; "this is our ticket home". He asked me to stand on it so that he could calibrate my biological systems into the machine, I did not really get what he was on about but I agreed nonetheless.

I stood on the device. He raised his left arm and a row of small lights appeared to hover above it and using the fingers on his right hand pressed into the lights and as he did a kind of static shock ran through me quite painless though, and simultaneously what I would describe as a dim light moved up down and seemingly all around me from my feet to my head.

"There, we're done, that didn't hurt a bit did it?"

I stepped off and asked him what the contraption was, he grinned exposing his bright dull looking teeth, he told me not too reluctantly that the machine was discovered in a crashed vessel used by the enemy. He said he was a science officer and linguist and one of the few who were able to decipher it.

"I and a colleague were sent on this mission, he didn't make it though, his name was Malcolm, an imminent linguist he specialized on psyphers hidden within ancient glyphs. Our world is older than yours, and it had gone through countless eras and many generations upon generations of inhabitants have lived and died on it, some came and went through the passage of history with little or no evidence of their civilization having ever existed, while others truly left indelible marks seen from buried art or literature, and structures hidden far below the surface and sometimes deep within the ocean floor discovered by chance by miners or explorers.

"My now dead colleague Malcolm and I were very talented in the field of psyphers, we had together deciphered many hidden truths, we created a computer prgramme that allows one to understand any language through emotion, we found that emotions were universal and our programme took on a life of its own plotting and mapping the entire sphere of emotion, and in essence applied it to every known language.

"When this devise was found on the downed ship, it was brought to both our attention, we had about reached a point in our battle, the point of giving up. Most of our engineered troops (cybers) had been defeated and or destroyed; it was just us Etherite marines and a few cybers left to defend our world.

"Unfortunately due to our initial use of Malcolm's settings many souls were lost, those were the bodies you encountered. He was among the first to come through the singularity, and unfortunately, as you know they didn't make it."

I knew that if I melded with him I would get all the information I needed, but I stopped myself, I didn't want to abuse the ability I would use it when it was really needed, instead I would use the information they wanted to give me, the information they would volunteer.

He was no longer grinning, I decided to leave.

I left the room in order to reconnect with Staff Seargent Ayeesha bell.

I asked her to teach me of her world and of the ways of those she called the unspoken. She said that this is what Colonel Handler, her Commanding Officer had just mandated her to do, she was ordered to debrief me on what I needed to know of the ways of Ether.

Ether

Ether is a world composed of 60% water and 40% land; it is the third planet from the sun within our solar cycle. The planet has been in existence for eons.

Ayeesha said "We human beings are ethereal we are made up of our surroundings; we are 80 % water based". She went on to say that the gravity on Gruce is heavier than it is on Ether, that this was why they were forced to wear their funny looking suits.

"Our boots are anti-gravitational they allow us to move more freely here."

"We rely more on technology than your kind do, I haven't seen or heard any form of vehicles or machinery of any kind since we arrived on your planet. You have no satellites or ships, no submersibles or aero transports. Your kind is truly independent of technology."

I grinned and scratched my chin, I knew our technology at Grubstone, or any of our piping stations would probably surpass anything on their planet.

She went on to tell me more about Ethers beginnings.

"In the AD15013, approximately 25,000 years ago a missing continent was discovered, it had been submerged for thousands of years its name is Lemuria, stone tablets were discovered, and on these tablets was so much information detailing the lemurian cultures and technological achievements. And From this information we were able to make so many breakthroughs in our own sciences, the lemurian culture existed long before ours but they were more advanced than ours. We translated most of the information retrieved, and from it we were able to harness the power of the tachyons, and this was the beginning of our evolution.

"For thousands of years after mastering the atom, splitting and merging of the atom were commonplace there was free energy we were able to create stars on ether and harness the energy that they possessed, shortly after these advancements there was a global food shortage. A consensus was reached by the world union for exploring other means for food creation, the world's scientific community was encouraged by way of grants given to them for DNA research in order to find a solution to end the food drought.

"Scientists applied similar techniques applied by nuclear physicists to atoms, on the organic genome, soon they were able to effect changes to DNA at a sub atomic level, and they were able to manipulate the molecular structure of the organic gene in any which way they needed.

"Soon they were able to fix the food problem. Crops became abundant because now they could grow almost anywhere, the cost of food plummeted.

"A few of scientists we called the renegades that still had grant generated finances would use it for their own personal unsanctioned research, they decided to take the technology gained, up a few notches, they would experiment on animal life, one renegade by the name of Doctor Norman was able to reawaken many creatures long since extinct, he unlocked what he coined the geneum blue print, a fundamental formula for the creation of animal life, it was like gaining access to a cheat code for the most difficult puzzle ever created.

"With his breakthrough they were able to reverse-engineer animal DNA on a molecular level and in essence break it apart and put it back together again.

"With this he unlocked the secret to creating DNA combinations, the basic building blocks of life. As you could imagine many religious groups were not happy with the idea of human beings now having the ability to create life, there were mass protests when the findings were leaked to the media. The doctor had hoped to improve on creation as a whole. From this innovation Doctor Hanson believed he could modify the human race, creating humans that are stronger, smarter and immune to sickness.

"Generations of research in the field of sub atomic mechanics went into this method of splitting and coupling of atoms. He wrote papers where he theorized about tampering with the human genome.

After about a decade Norman designed the first hybrid animal, it was a combination of two of Ethers most ferocious felines the lion and the tiger, he called this hybrid a Liger, it was bigger and stronger than both its forefathers but much more docile. He opened the hearts of the people of Ether to the possibility of us becoming benevolent entities with the power to create life, not by birth but by innovation.

"After his death many gained access to his work, mainly by sanction of the military complex, corporations were interested in his research and wanted the power to take his work in whichever direction they saw fit, one man by the name of Doctor Mustafa Nassim, a name now synonymous with death, pain and destruction, created the first of the chimera, this was the catalyst which fueled the burning embers of the age old holy war between the army and the knights.

"Mustafa had gained so much wealth from his giant strides in genetic science. He was able to take Dr Normans research much further and to fuse human DNA with the genetic material of other creatures, some long since extinct, like the scourge a flesh eating specie of animal originating from mars.

"During an expedition in the Mars colony, a fossil was found, it was carbon dated to 1 million years, it was brought back to earth for further research, somehow Mustafa gained access to the fossil, the story goes that he took it back to his lab, there he was able to salvage its genetic material, he merged it with the cells of an African croc, the croc is a reptile and the fossil looked reptilian, scaly according to him. His lab was in the continent of South America in a place called Columbia many miles underground.

"The creature was engineered with some human DNA there, in a short time, about a year it grew too big for the facility to contain it, they planned to move it while it was tranquilized, but no matter how much it was given it would not go down, at almost twenty feet tall and thirty feet wide, it broke out of its containment. It caused so much damage."

As he went on describing the beast the more it reminded me of the Grubbers at Grubstone, could this beast have been a Grubber. He went on to tell me that once the beast had gotten on the surface it caused such damage, to lives and property there were so many dead it appeared to be headed towards the sea, all the damage was done on its way there. It took a world resolution to stop it which had to be reached in order to sanction the application of weapons, banned by the world union, because of their detrimental effect on the environment. These were chem/bio weapons and this was what finally neutralized it. The weapons were used for three days and over ten thousand lost souls later, before the creature finally fell.

I began to understand why they needed us Regimentarians to help them in their war, it took them so long to destroy a Grubber-like beast something that when morphed we destroy in seconds, and with my new abilities I could destroy them in nanoseconds.

While on trial for the murder of the victims Mustafa reminded us of all the good his research had done for mankind, during the food scarcity, but in the end the judges still sentenced him to death, for all the innocents that had lost their lives to his creation.

On Ether the death sentence one carries out on oneself. On the day of his sentence after an elaborate and apologetic speech his last words were "THERE ARE NO GODS BUT WE FEW, FLAWED AND WEAK WE FEW ARE." he then took the poison and died.

"Dr Ling, a student of Mustafa, considered a God among the geneum community today, he was the best of Mustafas protégées. Over 5,000years later he is still highly revered on Ether.

"He was able to do so much for us humans, he created treatments which expanded the human life span, we now average three hundred years and due to treatments we have conquered so many limitations.

"Dr ling was able to take Mustafas research and improve on it such that it was very advantageous to our kind.

"Dr ling was a visionary and he believed that there was more to our own existence, than what we thought to be possible. He would visit ancient sites in hotter northern regions, after the polar caps melted during the sixth flood a millennia ago, a wealth of hidden, never before seen fossils and artifacts were found, including scrolls and artifacts from long dead civilizations.

"Dr Ling was against the maxim which stated that, history shall always repeat itself. Though his bio-sciences almost eradicated hunger on Ether, he engineered a formulae - a program, a combination, not a code, it was more like a constantly changing organic algorithm morphing evolving to suit its surrounding, it was an improvement to Dr Norman's work: crops now had the ability to grow where they normally wouldn't be able too, they could change their structure and adapt to the limitations of their locations. It was genius. This program was called the game changer gene or the adapter gene.

"Doctor Ling adapted it to the human race, but because of the world resolution reached after Hanson's chimera incident; which made it unlawful for anyone to engage in any experiments whatsoever to do with the hybridization of the human race; Dr ling was only able to theorize about the possibility of creating a perfect man, one that would be totally immune to all disease, much stronger due to increase in the tensile strength of his muscle fibers and so on, also very intelligent due to the increase in his nervous synaptic relay systems. In essence some that possessed these qualities would also possess the ability to know without knowing: a power the ancients the AMERIKANS called clairvoyance. Dr ling was an esoteric thinker, he was very much a scientist with an open mind, he researched into civilizations of Ethers past. There mystical practices and there sciences. Most of his research into this realm of thought was secret. He said most of his inspiration came from these ancient civilizations. He often spoke of the continent of Lemuria and Atlantis, he collected so much information, he valued the so called star charts of the Anak more than everything. It was believed that this is where he found the coordinates to this planet and others. You call your planet Gruce, and Dr Ling called it planet X

"Dr Ling disappeared for close to one hundred years; we all presumed he had become a recluse because that was the nature of most eccentric scientists. But it was during the arrival that humans understood what he had worked on. He had information about the unspoken, he researched on them, and prepared for their return. From ancient tablets and esoteric mystic practice he was able to know about their ways and their capacity. It was from this knowledge that he created your species. Your sole purpose in life is to prepare for the arrival of the unspoken. Your kind are were to be our secret weapon on their return.

"I am an example of Dr lings legacy, I am a bionic, or what is known as a cyber, an enhanced human being bred for soldiering, I bleed and have normal human functions but I am much stronger, I am sure you can remember from our first encounter, I can take a licking but keep on ticking!"

The Arrival

"The human race had come so far, technologies had become a very important part of life on Ether. There was no longer disease or famine, all the plagues had been conquered, and our only bane on Ether was war.

"The religious conflict that has been ongoing for longer than I can remember.

"The planet was stable and generally its inhabitants were happy, but for the war, it caused such disunity among us. The Army and the knights fought each other over differences in ideologies and beliefs. They fought to the death; it was a never ending cycle of pain, and destruction.

"It was all about to change, for it is said that only a common enemy can unite former foes.

"It was during the arrival that the army and the knights put to bed all enmity and united a world divided in order to better defend it against a new threat.

"The arrival was the day that changed it all, an answer to the burning question, are we alone in the universe was so emphatically answered, in a most bitter and terrible manner.

"They are the Unspoken because after the arrival the mere mention of them was to invoke a fear, one that was palpable and heavy.

"These unspokens have been called many names through the passage of Ether,s histories, which include Annunaki, and the gods of bygone ages.

"We have been able to gather the following information directly from these beings themselves, in or about 50,000bc humans were designed and genetically modified by others.

"They arrived in the gulf near the Euphrates River.

"There was said to be a high concentration of certain elements found in the river and sea waters of that area. These special beings were interested in these elements, and humans were modified by them to work as slaves, they needed humans to mine these elements for them. The elements were said to possess special properties that could enhanced and repair all bodily functions and stop the body from aging.

"The humans on Ether back then were not like us, they were more passion driven and less rational. Their brains were not developed as much as our present day human beings, in fact fossil remains have shown that their cerebellums were much smaller, so small that their brains were only slightly bigger than that of lesser animals.

"The visitors used them as slaves for centuries.

"The legend goes that one day a water holder a female of these earlier species of human noticed a sliver of an object glittering on the floor. She bent down and picked it up. She palmed it, made a fist around it and took it to her cave that evening. She decided to eat it, she would chew bits of it every day, and soon it was totally consumed by her.

"On a random day one of her tribesmen had his way with her, soon she was pregnant, it would be a boy, he was born, but this boy came out a bit different than all the others, and as the years rolled by his looks and character had set him apart from all the others, if Dr Ling had been there he would have said the boy was the first game changer gene for the human race. I thought this was much like the pull up programme of Arbonan.

"The elements the mother had ingested had bonded with her and she passed it down to her boy. It had inadvertently evolved the human race through this boy, as you could say he was the first true human.

"The others, the slaves the ones who had been mining and building structures in reverence of the unspoken, decided to revolt, and they were systematically wiped out.

"Our first of many had been monitored by the unspoken for some time, they copied his model and genetically modified the entire human race to that effect, only that this time they weoponised the element, it was released into the atmosphere like a pathogen, particularly targeting humans only, it would bond with the women folk and at the same time reduce their life span, they could only live for 2 years after this.

"By today's standards biological attack, the fathers would live to raise the children. These Adamic children, the golden ones of our beginnings, had a more advance cerebral system, with higher cognitive awareness than the first breed, they were more easily controlled and manipulated.

"They multiplied and they travelled to regions farther away and evolved through the ages. The ways in which they evolved depended on the nature of their surroundings, those in the temperate hotter regions evolved into darker skin tones and those in the less temperate regions grew lighter and as time went on their facial structures also adapted to their surroundings, those that migrated through the dusty deserts adapted slanty eyes brought about by many years of squinting and so on.

The father of evolution theory Darwin explained these phenomena in his Canary Island findings. This is how the races on Ether were born, through millennia of changes upon changes and so forth.

"The visitors would come to us during the early stages of our creation many ages ago, they were worshipped as gods; these were the gods of Mayan empire, the gods of Egyptians, the gods of the Sumerians, the gods of the Germans and of the Romans.

They were the gods whom idols were based on; the gods that pyramids, like the Giza, machu pichu, and tiwanaka were dedicated to. These were the root of all grim creatures that have haunted us through our childhood, the ones from the stories our parents read to us as children, all nightmare creatures. The unspoken were the root of all this.

"It was said that when the first ship breached the atmosphere. There was celebration and jubilation throughout all of Ether, they were told of a glorious end of days and of the judgment to come. The ship was about 1000 meters in circumference, it was a golden floating disc. As it emerged through the clouds. The best of our military minds were set to establish what it was and from whence it came. It stayed motionless for precisely 30 days, in the same position, with just a faint hum that could be heard everywhere of which the military believed was the sound of its engines. At first the military planned for the worst case scenario. They tried to breach it, they bombed and lasered it. It remained motionless and seemingly unscathed; it must have a shield of sorts.

"After two weeks of trying to bring it down the military had failed.

"It remained there ominous like some benevolent object with the ability to survive whatever was thrown at it.

"On the thirtieth day, the official day contact was made between Etherlings and the Unspoken.

"The faint hum stopped, and almost instantaneously, all communications on Ether failed. No I view signals, radio waves, rim networks, and all of Ether,s over 10,000 satellites orbiting the planet failed.

"This lasted about an hour but in this time aero transports crashed, snake lines and bird lines had crashed thousands had been killed and countless ones injured. But within the space of that hour the satellites and the networks came up again and as fast as they were up they had shut down. A message which was played simultaneously on every frequency and I view station.

"The message was a mild voice basically narrating the story I explained earlier, about them being our creators.

At the end of the history lesson they ordered all nations to submit to them by offering prayers and sacrifices to them, like our forefathers had done in the past.

"The world union resolved that the threat was not as bad as it appeared.

"You see they overlooked the fact that this object had appeared out of nowhere, there was no advance notice of its breaching Ether,s atmosphere. There ships were equipped with the same tech we are going to use to send you and you brothers in arms to Ether. The ships are equipped with singular portation devices. Instruments that create singularities or space windows they can move through that allow them to leap frog the many light years distances of space so as to easily move from planet to planet.

"Our generals neglected these facts. They believed this was the only ship. They were fool hardy.

"Over a thousand similar such ships appeared at an instant from which thousands of beings – shadow reapers - tall dark grayish scaly creatures with big black brooding eyes, were beamed down to earth they looked like soulless creatures. As they appeared weapons in hand Ether's sanitization had begun; the unspoken had arrived, where ever they appeared death would follow. It was a campaign of complete obliteration, they wanted to wipe us humans out the same way they did Neanderthals their first creations.

"They had come back to Ether much later in history, we humans had reached a level of sophistication they were not prepared for we fought back with our armies our technologies and with our hearts. We fought back by sacrificing our own. In areas that were heavily overrun by these creatures nuclear devises were used but no matter what damage we did their numbers did not seem to dwindle, but ours did for where there were 100,000 human souls and 1,000 of the unspoken were present we would use nuclear, and or bio/chem. Weapons to destroy them and our human losses would be counted as collateral damage.

"This battle had gone on for so long that the number of purebred humans has significantly reduced. And now most of Ether has been colonized by these creatures, they have already established mining sites, like they had so many thousands of years before.

"Dr Ling, had used his great genius so many thousands of years ago to create your species he was able to finance the program of growing your kind in test tubes, as a controllable option if something like this was to occur. Your planet Gruce was a massive big brother experiment that has taken place for over 10,000 years. Gruce was terraformed and tailor-designed.

The same way the unspoken engineered the human race was the same way Dr Ling engineered planet X or Gruce.

"Draemen we will be at par with the aliens with the help of you and your comrades' in this our last effort to regain Ether's freedom, we have a fighting chance!"

Reunification

Ayesha had so eloquently brought me abreast of the real issues and now I have a fresh idea of what lies ahead.

I see Sergeant Blade a few meters away by the broak tree. He sees me too and we exchange smiles, I walk towards him and in a loud voice I ask him if he knows when we will be leaving, he answers me back loudly, and that we leave when my Gruce and I are ready.

I was sure that Taek would be the first to arrive because of the proximity to my farm from his office.

I walked through the backdoor into my dwelling, I thought now would be a good time to relax and take stock of the events that have unfolded in these very few days. I got into my sleeping room, my mind still thinking on the debriefing I was just given by Ayesha, a self confessed cyber. I believed she would be an adequate guide to me and the regiment once we arrived at our destination.

I always left a bucket of bath water in my bathing room, and it was still there, but unlike Grubstone it was cold, we use what we call ground stones, these are stones of manganese and sulfur, they cause a reaction in the water which create heat the water doesn't get as hot as the ones from the piping station though, just less cold. I pop the stone in the bucket, and watch as the reaction occurs the water fizzes and shortly settles.

I sit on the bath bench and use the pail to pour the now warm water on my head and shoulders I scrub in the gels they lather and I washed them off and in a short while I was done.

I usually dry myself naturally, I don't have blowers.

I looked in the mirror and noticed I had increased my muscle mass, I was more defined, my chest, shoulders and abs were more pronounced, I then noticed that I actually felt fitter and more energetic than usual, these pull ups really do their work, I was beginning to look more like the moon worshippers of Arbonan.

I arranged my gear on my bed then I went to my store room where I kept most of my stuff, I never usually use weapons, but I have been collecting and training with them on my spare time for some time now.

I had a choice of staffs, spears, and, and array of swords. The mission for which I was bound, was a combative one in which I knew there would be casualties, and I knew that I had to exact as many casualties on the enemy, the Shadow Reapers, as possible. Marcsor my father was a master swordsman, a weilder regimentarian of the highest order he was the last of the wielders. And as a boy I did watch him train on this land,

I watched and I studied, but it was only after his death that I took on training on the way of the sword proper. Lango Lis my sensai taught me the art of sword play, he taught to think through the sword he showed me how to make the sword an extension of my spirit.

One of the twelve was a sword wielder by the name of sensai Takeshi Tano; his works on sword play made us all fear and respect the power of the sword, he was the father of swordplay on Gruce.

Lango Lis was from a long line of sensai Takeshi students. Of all the swords in my store I stare at one, the one I put aside the one I kept on its own. Lango Lis had gifted this one to me. On the day of my fathers ashing, he told me that my father was his mentor and that he was a great sword wielder, and he pledged that he would train me on that day. Even though wielding was no longer on the curriculum of study. He told me that all sword weilders must name their sword because even though a sword is to be an extention of your spirit it also has a spirit of its own and therefore a name must follow.

Lango Lis told me its name, he called this sword Unbendable. Now so many years later I was again close to the sword I had just been through the pull up program and just newly mastered the five telekinetic senses, I fealt a presence a consciousness in the room with me and for some reasone that feeling emanated from the sword, I stood about five feet away from it, I looked in its and I called its name and extended my sword hand, my right hand out and the sword moved slightly I shouted its name "unbendable" it rose up of the wall, I concentrated I willed it to unsheathe itself and it did, it shot out of its sheath and hovered in the air the sheath fell to the floor; the sword hovered towards me its white ivory blade was glowing and a soothing hum permeated the air, the sweet sound came from the sword I exposed my palm to it and it turned slowly right side up and seemingly connected to my hand, as it did, wrapping my fist around it I clasped the handle tightly. I felt it meld with me and suddenly 200 cycles of the skills of its former masters were embedded into me I fealt my Fthers spirit too, it was a wealth of knowledge, much more than anything I ever learnt from Lango Lis.

I ran out of the store to the frontage where it all happened, as I stepped out the snow I began performing sword katas I had never ever seen not to mention perform.

I swung left and right under and over in varying ways till I ended up upside down performing a sword stand, just like my father did when he was alive I then understood why Lango Lis called this sword 'unbendable'. I planted it in the snowy floor and performed a hand stand while holding it, the sword carried the brunt of my weight, and did not bend.

This was what my father told me of as a child, the joining of a psychomat and a ronin, tekeshi called them dynastic warriors, and this was a legend passed down to then weilder Regimentarians through many cycles by Tekeshi. Warriors that fought not with their weapons but alongside them. As I righted myself I saw them land one by one in front of me, first Nenveve, then Trool and then Taek.

Finally we were reunited.

To be contd...

Lightning Source UK Ltd.
Milton Keynes UK
UKOW04n1955170316

270417UK00002B/27/P